For each of these magnificent and delightful birds:
Kai, Lucia, Ella, Rowan, Lillian, Bennett, Leo, Abby,
Julian, Nina, Joaquin, Marcel, Katy, Quinn, Gus,
and Opal —M.M.

To my friends and family, who never put me in a box.
Thank you for giving me the room to shake my feathers
and fly. —K.J.

THIS IS A BORZOI BOOK PUBLISHED BY ALFRED A. KNOPF

Text copyright © 2021 by Megan Maynor
Jacket art and interior illustrations copyright © 2021 by Kaylani Juanita

Visit us on the Web! rhcbooks.com

Educators and librarians, for a variety of teaching tools, visit us at RHTeachersLibrarians.com

Library of Congress Cataloging-in-Publication Data is available upon request.
ISBN 978–1–9848–9648–3 (trade) — ISBN 978–1–9848–9649–0 (lib. bdg.) — ISBN 978–1–9848–9650–6 (ebook)

The text of this book is set in 17–point Memo Pro and 21–point Nouveau Crayon.
The illustrations were created digitally using multimedia.
Book design by Nicole Gastonguay

MANUFACTURED IN CHINA

February 2021
10 9 8 7 6 5 4 3 2 1
First Edition

A HoUSE for EVERY BiRD

by
MEGAN MAYNoR

iLLustrations by
KAYLANI JUANiTA

Alfred A. Knopf
New York

I drew all these birds.
And a house for every bird.
Doo-be-doo.

Red for red,

tall for tall.

A house
for one,
a house
for all . . .
Ta-dah!

What are you doing, Blue Bird?
That house is not for you.

Oh no, this is THE house for me. Orange is my color! So bold! So bright! Full of light! Like me!

But you're blue.

Only on the outside.

What? That doesn't make sense. I'm just going to step in here and put you back where you belong.

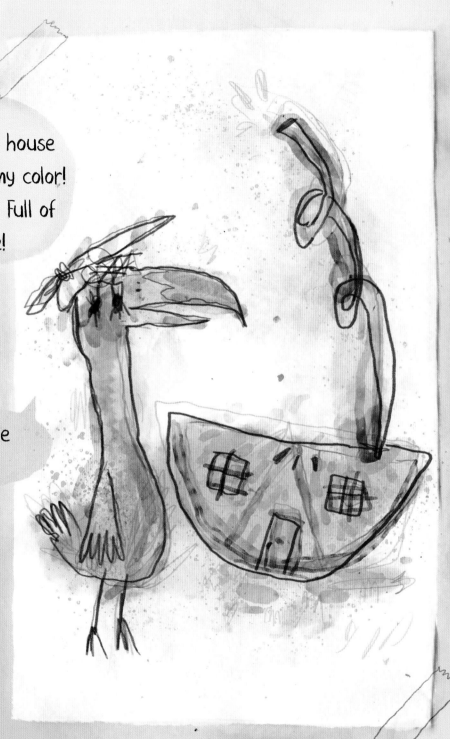

Hey! Small Bird! What are you doing in that large house? *Shoo! Shoo!*

let me tell you. I have a whole flock of cousins. We are in a singing group together and our act is HUGE! We will fill this place up.

But that's not fair to Large Bird. He can't live in a small house.

Um, hi. I get worried in big spaces. I feel much better in this small house, where I can touch all the walls at once. Please don't yell at me.

Okay, but that's enough. I am the boss
here and I say NO MORE SWITCHING.
Maybe I should've used tape. Where's
my glue stick?

No. NO. NO!
You have it all wrong!
Ducks like ponds.
Parakeets like swings.

Not this duck.

I don't swim, man.

Nor this parakeet.

UGH! WHAT IS GOING ON IN THIS NEIGHBORHOOD? Birds, you need to stay where I put you. Everybody STAY! Stay . . . stay . . .

But I was trying to help.
I made a house for
every bird. How was
I supposed to KNOW
what you like?

Ask us.

Oh.

But I thought
I knew—

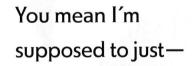
Ask us!

You mean I'm
supposed to just—

ASK US!

Okay . . . Uh, Green Bird?
You're still in the green
house. What kind of
house do you want?

I'm good.

I guess you really can't tell a bird by its feathers.

And the only way
to know a bird is . . .
to get to know a bird.

Okay, I'm gonna make some
bird food. *Doo-be-doo.*
Seeds for one, seeds for all . . .
Wait—does every bird like seeds?

I prefer nuts!